ALFIE'S Great Escape

Kate Irwin

Illustrated by Clare Elsom

Reading Ladder

A baboon called Alfie fell out with his best friend Toby.

'I'm fed up of being a baboon!' said
Alfie to himself. 'I wish I lived with
humans! *They're* never mean.
They never fall out with each other.'

Alfie knew this because he saw lots of humans every day. He sat on their cars as they drove round the safari park.

He watched them smiling and chatting
and eating ice cream.

'I know!' said Alfie. 'If I collect lots of bits off the *humans'* cars, I can put them all together and make my *own* car! And I can drive away to join the humans!'

So, that's just what Alfie did.

Alfie built his own car.

He jumped in, and he started it up.

'Hurray!' he said, and drove out of the
safari park.

Alfie drove down country lanes and
through villages.

He came to a house covered in balloons and banners.

Alfie stopped and went through the gate.

The house and garden were full of wild animals! Only they didn't look *quite* like wild animals.

12

'Welcome to our jungle party!' said a
Nice Lady. 'Come and join the fun!'

13

Alfie had fun on the bouncy castle.

He had fun on the swings.

And he had fun playing with some
toilet paper. (He found that upstairs.)

'Alfie!' exclaimed the Nice Lady. 'You
need to calm down!'

Alfie was having a marvellous time!
But then he saw something that
worried him.

A tiger and an antelope were fighting
over a frisbee.

But humans don't fight! thought Alfie.

'Are you just *pretending* to fight?'
he asked. 'Because that's what wild
animals do?'
'Get lost!' said Tiger, and pushed him.

Alfie thought Antelope needed some
help with pretending to fight . . .

They don't look like they are pretending!

. . . and the Nice Lady had to sit him in
a Quiet Corner of the Garden to Calm
Down.

'I know!' said Alfie to himself. 'I'll check
someone for fleas! That always calms
me down!'

'ARE YOU SAYING I'VE GOT
NITS??!' yelled Giraffe.
'You've got lots!' Alfie popped some
into his mouth. 'Yummy!'

Mmm!

'GET OFF!' yelled Giraffe,
and pushed him over.

Careful!

Alfie fell
backwards on
to Rhino.

'OW!' yelled
Rhino, and
whacked him
on the head.

Alfie pinned
her to the
floor.

The Nice Lady had to sit them in two
Quiet Corners of the Garden to Calm
Down.

Rhino sneaked over to Alfie and poked him.

'Where's my present?' she hissed.

'What present?' asked Alfie.

'*My birthday present, stupid!*'

'Oh . . .' said Alfie. 'I'll . . . get it in a minute.'

'Time for tea!' called the Nice Lady.

Rhino charged inside.

But Alfie stayed in the Quiet Corner of
the Garden.

What can I give Rhino as a present? he thought, as he munched on a beetle. *What would I like? Something nice to eat, perhaps . . .?*

I've got it!

The children started their jelly and ice cream. Alfie came in.

uh oh

'Here's your birthday present, Rhino!'
he said.

He plonked it down on the table.

Lots of beetles! And bugs! And worms!

And slugs!

'You're going to LOVE these!'

25

'AAAAAAAARGH!' screamed the
Birthday Girl. 'AAAAAAAAAARGH!'
The beetles and bugs and worms and
slugs jumped out of their skins and into
the jelly and ice cream.

'AAAAAAAAARGH!' screamed the
children. They threw the jelly and
ice cream and beetles and bugs and
worms and slugs far away from them.

They landed on the faces of the
children across the table.

'AAAAAAAAARGH!' they screamed.

And they threw it all back!

SPLIDGE! 'AAAAAAAAARGH!'

SPLODGE! 'AAAAAAAAAARGH!'

SPLAT! 'AAAAAAAAAAAAAARGH!'

The Birthday Girl stood up.

'I HATE YOU, YOU HORRIBLE MONKEY! YOU'VE RUINED MY BIRTHDAY PARTY! GET OUT!'

Alfie's head and shoulders drooped.
He slunk out of the house. He flopped
down on the grass and put his head in
his hands.

Antelope, Zebra and Cheetah followed.
'Don't be sad, Alfie!' they said.
'But I wrecked Rhino's party!' said
Alfie. 'And she hates me! She even
called me a *monkey*!'

'But it was the Best Party Ever!'
said the others.

'You wrapped me in loo roll!'
said Cheetah.

'You saved me from
a bully!' said
Antelope.

'And we had a Fantabulous Food Fight!' said Zebra.

'Will you come to MY birthday party?'

'And mine?'

'And mine?'

Alfie felt a big lump in his throat. He gave them all a big baboon hug.

Then he felt better.

'Shall I say sorry to Rhino?' he asked.

Alfie said sorry to Rhino.

Rhino scowled

at him.

Then she smiled. 'It's okay,' she said.

'Would you like some birthday cake?' said the Nice Lady.
'Can I take some home for Toby?' asked Alfie. 'He's my best friend.'

'Course you can,' the Nice Lady said.

And Alfie smiled a Big Baboon Smile.

At home-time, Alfie went to find
his car.

He drove back through the safari park.

Lions lazed in the sun.

Reindeer nuzzled each other.

And baboons played tag.

Then they chilled out, and checked each other for fleas.

43

'TOBY!' cried Alfie. He ran and gave Toby a Big Hug.

'I'm sorry I was silly! Can we be friends again?' Alfie asked.

'Of course we can!' said Toby. 'I've missed you, Alfie!'

Alfie and Toby *sometimes* fell out after that.

And sometimes Alfie went to a Quiet Corner of the Safari Park to Calm Down.

But they always made up.

And Alfie kept his car, just in case he needed it.